LAND OF SUPERIOR MIRAGES

JOHNS HOPKINS: POETRY AND FICTION
John T. Irwin, General Editor

Adrien Stoutenburg

LAND OF SUPERIOR MIRAGES

New and Selected Poems

edited by DAVID R. SLAVITT

with a foreword by JAMES DICKEY

THE JOHNS HOPKINS UNIVERSITY PRESS
Baltimore and London

This book has been brought to publication with the generous assistance
of the G. Harry Pouder Fund and the Albert Dowling Trust.

© 1986 The Johns Hopkins University Press
All rights reserved
Printed in the United States of America

The Johns Hopkins University Press
701 West 40th Street
Baltimore, Maryland 21211
The Johns Hopkins Press Ltd., London

The paper used in this publication meets the minimum
requirements of American National Standard for Infor-
mation Sciences—Permanence of Paper for Printed
Library Materials, ANSI Z39.48. 1984.

Library of Congress Cataloging-in-Publication Data

Stoutenburg, Adrien.
  Land of superior mirages.

  (Johns Hopkins, poetry and fiction)
  I. Slavitt, David R., 1935–   . II. Title. III. Series.
PS3569.T67L3   1986   811'.54   85-45862
ISBN 0-8018-3335-3 (alk. paper)
ISBN 0-8018-3336-1 (pbk.: alk. paper)

Some poems in this volume were previously published in
Heroes, Advise Us (Charles Scribner's Sons), *Short History
of the Fur Trade* (Houghton Mifflin), and *Greenwich
Mean Time* (University of Utah Press); "Achilles,"
"The Allergic," "Avalanche," and excerpts from "This
Journey" and "Short History of the Fur Trade" first appeared
in *The New Yorker*.

Contents

Foreword

I never met Adrien Stoutenburg, nor had I ever heard of her until I
served as a judge, one year, for a national literary prize; her book
Short History of the Fur Trade was brought to my attention by
another judge, W. H. Auden, and immediately became my candidate
for the prize. It did not win, but my personal admiration for her
poetry began, from which point it continued, and increased.

Out of sources entirely her own, Adrien Stoutenburg projects a
morality that, once encountered, becomes an unshakable part of the
reader's conscience. If I were to characterize the tone of voice, I
would call it that of sensitive outrage, quivering, powerful, and
delicate. Delicate: *therefore* powerful, and many times more
memorable than mere bludgeoning or screaming; the human rape of
the natural world comes through with shocking and profound
impact, and her sense of personal violation at the destruction of
nonhuman life, of the unreproducible *forms* of existence. Love for
these destroyed mysteries is matched by the poet's hatred of the
destroyers—agencies, hardly people—who swap life for money, like
John Jacob Astor and the profiteering of his Hudson Bay Company
from animal-slaughter. In an age when irony is much esteemed, her
form of it is particularly creative and highly individual; nothing about
it is standard, everything unexpected and telling. In this passage, for
example, the animals end; here their beauty, or some of it, is
transferred to people in the form of garments, the sickening profit
made.

> The ocelot, bright black and gold,
> is stacked in heaps, torn from Bolivia
> and breath. The snow leopard, stretched and groomed,
> makes a rug so deep, the appraiser's fingers
> sleep in it, reluctant to wake;
> so warm, it seems still wrapped around a heart
> beating against the blue Himalayan frost.
> The jaguar, mottled with pansies,
> hangs from a hook beside the lynx and headless wolf,
> all thirst and pain removed,
> insured against mildew, moths, and thieves.

The women who make the Trade possible are not spared, nor their insistence on the sacrifice of living creatures for as ignoble an idea as fashion; re-created but not chastened, they hoist the lifeless and resplendent hides onto their backs, put their arms through the holes of the sleeves, and turn to the nearest image of themselves. The women's part of the animal-holocaust ends in the show-room; it takes place in the mirror.

> The cheetah's silk, though it does not wear as well
> as the leopard's flowing cloth, is "sportier"
> among those who peddle such intense brocades.
> Tiger skin, indelibly marked
> by shafts of light and shade,
> needs a special female type
> to bear its wild embroidery—
>   skinny, tall, with a feline slant
>   around the eyes, cheekbones, or teeth.
>
> Mountain lions, for all their grace, are difficult,
> the color, like a red-brown sunset, harsh;
> recommended strictly for casual dress—
> ski slopes, winter golf, a northern beach,
> or race tracks when the chill is deep enough.

In a famous essay Stephen Spender confesses that as a poet he lacks confidence in using his memory to create situations outside himself; that he cannot remember imaginatively his own felt experiences so as "to know what it is like to explore the North Pole." The kind of imaginative projection where Spender feels he is weak is exactly where Adrien Stoutenburg is strongest. In her long poem "This Journey" she seeks, with Robert Falcon Scott and his companions, not the North Pole but the South, and with an imaginative energy matched by few poets at any time, in any language.

> The last expedition is never the last
> and loaves of frost are never divided
> into a multitude of fishes,
> and the skua must feed on the kidney he finds
> or the eyes that come like a light to meet him
> in his hunger-darkness. The hooked beak drives
> all but speech into the waste

of breaking tumblers and grinding patterns,
and words are written.

> *The small green tent and the great white road . . .*
> *The hiss of the primus . . .*
> *The whine of the dog . . .*
> *The neigh of our steeds . . .*
> *The driving cloud of powdered snow . . .*
>
> *Two minutes in the open makes a white figure . . .*

Stoutenburg's approach to the long poem is as individual as her choice of details. Her intense and sad—and quite American—surrealism takes surprisingly well to narrative, and her story-sense is remarkable, productive of momentum and tragic inevitability.

It would be difficult to read through this collection without being struck by the resilience and resourcefulness of Stoutenburg's imagination, its sheer encompassment. It can be turned upon—or well up from—anything from a dog-skin rug to the grave of Yeats, in the latter case in terms Yeats might not have liked, but whose prideful insistence on individual outlook, not to be cowed for one instant by the outlook or words of the great, he could not have ignored.

> No horseman I,
> but still a rider through rain and green
> and dusk, casting a cold eye.

I think often of the woeful neglect of this woman, of the marvelous creative intellect that earned a living as a small-town librarian, and under various pseudonyms by writing children's books, mysteries, and travelogs, and of Adrien Stoutenburg's time spent, during her terrible battle with esophogeal cancer, in various hospitals and intensive care units, full of life near its suffering close, the special life that only the dying have. From one of these she protested

> With the tube down my throat
> I could not tell them.

Now is the time for the telling. Now, and from now on.

JAMES DICKEY

NEW POEMS

Next Door to the Rest Home Laundry

Even before the sparrow's cranky dawn,
the machines begin to drone,
grind against sleep, surround me
like a metal swarm.

I visualize bed sheets,
soiled gowns, and yellowed socks
(night-sweats, cold phlegm,
still hanging in their folds)
awash in steaming rainbows
of White King or Tide.

The dryer spins with headless things
that tumble in its turning drum. Above the din
young laundresses sing,
gossip and babble
with Spanish-fluted tongues.

An ambulance rackets to a halt
and something on a stretcher is hustled away.
Once more, the laundry shed
groans into life. I am bound to praise
such rites of cleanliness,

but must old squatter death,
waiting its chance to leap,
make such a noise and fuss of it
while I (as even the sparrows must)
cling to the perch of ordinary sleep?

Before We Drown

I have seen myself and others
rolling in this ocean,
and the arrows of fish in the surf,
and a shark walking upon the water,
and Noah sailing with trumpets,
and a giraffe limping ashore
like a mottled tree.

We are here to salute the sea,
to taste salt, to burn our eyes
with sunlight and the black smoke of driftwood
started from one match against the headlines.

We are here to measure waves
and the length of the marlin's gill
and to gather up into castles
the wandering, witless sand
before the tide turns
and we see our dead selves
mirrored, open-mouthed,
in its glass shoulders.

Listening to the Silence

Nature, that great, green, glorified idiot,
cannot communicate, or does not want to.
The owl speaks to itself.
The ant is busy building barns.
The rain stammering on leaf and roof
is a gray introvert.
Daylong, the buzzards, black-tongued,
gossip to each other
above a city of pines,
itself a babble of sighs
and untranslatable gestures.

They speak to themselves
when they bother to speak at all:
the bats that sometimes squeak
hang-gliding by my door at dusk;
the squirrel that curses me
(that much seems clear)
from trees I own as much as he;
the mole's deep whisper underground.

So be it. I can only try to interpret
the murmur, cry, or purr
in my own way. If I err,
let the wind or one of the other voices
speak out. I will try hard to hear.

Lures

for Charley

It was timber-raped land
in that high north,
the stumps of white pine left
like riddled tombs
in the midst of slash
and upstart, peasant jacks.
But in winter, long after
the mosquitoes' narrow whine,
our lakes were fat with ice
and food-keen pike.
                    We hunted them
in their cold palaces.
We is a braggart's term.
I was a child but I helped
when my grandfather
with heavy thumbs
and pipe-grooved lip
made his crude lures from whittled scrap.
They seemed to me high art,
those rigid minnow shapes
let down through green-blue circles
sawed in a fishhouse floor
to tempt the hungry gleams beneath.

Our rude bait swiveled, swam,
at the set line's end,
adorned with hooks.
They flashed like dreams of jewels,
their fins and tails cut from a coffee tin.
A bung of solder in the belly
weighed them down.
Mine was the final touch:
the burning-in with a redhot pick
of eyes and gills,

even an upturned mouth.
I was good at this, people said,
and I took pride.
                    I wonder now
how much my smiling decoys helped
to kill.
            What I remember—
and without guilt—
is the sweet flesh steaming on my plate
and how the old man and I,
in silence, bowed over it
and ate . . . and ate.

Memory Album

When this you see,
Remember me.

Memory is a miser, spendthrift, thief,
unearthing entire sepulchers,
blind cottonwoods, murmur of kitchen stoves,
geranium smell of musty living rooms,
the millinery sign that creaked
outside the shopworn house
where I read fairytales
while rain invented curtains on the wind.

Processions of farmers, merchants,
fishermen: a tramp with sooty eyes
at the back door, and wives with scattered hair
and soap-red hands;
old Bill, the ram, who butted when provoked,
tin cowbells beating in the pines,
the gasping freight below the water tank,
the depot where a metronome
clicked out its constant messages
of birthdays, marriages, and death.

I know each name. This one died on a train
(the scalpel showed a rusted heart):
another, lovelorn, blew his brains apart
rather than face a simpering girl's disdain;

and those with tumors, those with bitten nails;
widow, hustler, saint, the simple, and the sly,
fathers, cousins, friends, all with one cry:
"Remember me! Remember me!" The past exhales

their mingled breath, and even the hot scent
  of sunflowers wearing halos meant
  for loftier dieties. All images are bent
through time, and some most prized are fraudulent—

as mine may be. Remember this, if you remember me.

River Boat

It surprised the night and me
like a suburb of lights
gone suddenly adrift.
Its searching beam,
a long, white spy sent out ahead,
probed trees, backwashes, drunken logs,
set weeds on fire,
and dazzled even mud to sparks.

Ignorant of broader craft
than common rowboat or canoe,
I blinked like a desert toad,
and held my breath
as it drummed near,
its deliberate bulk
strung with electric fireflies
to warn the darkness from its path.

"An ordinary Mississippi barge,"
my river-wise companion said.

No. What glided there
was a fallen freight of stars
that put the wind ablaze
and burned—and stays.

Storm's Eye

The wind is over my head,
inside it,
and galloping everywhere
with leaves. Brown wrists of shrubs
are broken, the madrone's spine twisted.
In the wind-lash,
the wild drift of peeled bark,
gossamer wheel and whirl of seeds,
my eyelashes seem fringed with smoke
and the fronds of blown dandelions
through which the world looks
a lost white, a tempest of feathers.
The drift clings.

I am blowing toward the sun,
ankles and shoulders winged
like those of rash Icarus.
But when I arrive there
at the fire-ringed hub,
I shall not blaze any more fiercely
than I do here and now.

Summer Snow

The strawberry's leaves
are a green hand spread open,
holding up one small flower—
a snowflake that can bear
the red and ripening sun.

Oblique

The palm tree beside my fence
has many voices: rain sometimes,
more often a sound of dry laths
clapping together as in applause
for the performing wind.

At times, catching the movement
of the fronds from an angle, aslant,
I think somebody, a person,
is gesturing there.

I may not be far wrong
although I'm not prepared to swear
to anything, being too partisan
of all that's made from sun and cloud
and leaf. Such things
when wind and mind are right
take on shapes more guessed at
by a glancing view than truly seen,
yet seeming more true; a way of looking
that can change a simple tree
to something keener, closer,
almost kin.

Absurd, I know, and not to be relied upon.
Only, I do.

Schopenhauer and the Orangutan

He wept for the sorrows of an ape,
that man of the forests and wild leaves
imprisoned at a Frankfurt fair,
and wondered if the creature there
was chained by its own shriveled will
or by the unbending will of bars.

The eyes, blood-brown, reminded him
of that red planet astronomers spied
in drafty space, although the beast
was merely finite stuff misshaped
into the mournful likeness of a man.

The world as will, he wrote,
is also the world as my idea.
His forehead bulged with ponderous thought;
the other's slanted, a narrow attic place
for an unfinished mind
which groped to understand
the frock-coated shape that stared at him,
until, half-shy, the crude beast turned
and hid its face in its long, bearded hands.

Crowds and carousels were loud,
a racketing menagerie.
Arthur abominated noise
and all the common, hammering world;
only the will-less dead were wise.
Misogynist and crank, fearful of barbers, thieves,
he studied the silent orang, and grieved,
before he walked in his own silence home.

Two boardinghouse rooms sufficed for him,
his pen, his poodle, books, and flute.
The pet dog fluttered at his feet,
a slave to comfort and easy food;

the master sat with brooding chin,
imagining a nest in a high branch,
great, dripping vines, a ghost-green moon,
and wrote another unyielding page.

At night, he gazed at the deep stars
and dreamed of distant Borneo, the earth-sweet rain,
a cloistered mate—then glimpsed
as on long nights before
the untidy crypt and zoo of love.
Again, in spite of will, he wept.

Intensive Care Unit

In one corner of the ward
somebody was eating a raw chicken.
The cheerful nurses did not see.
With the tube down my throat
I could not tell them.
Nor did they notice the horror show
on the TV set suspended over my windowless bed.
The screen was dead
but a torn face was clear.

I did not see my own
in a mirror for weeks.
When it happened,
when I dared to face my face
after the ravaging,
it was not mine
but something whittled, honed down
to a sly resemblance.
It, even the mirror, the pale room,
the oxygen tank
neat and black as a bomb
in its portable crate—
all was hallucination.

But the bloody rooster,
the stray pieces of bodies
slung into dreamless nooks,
the white-haired doll whimpering
on a gift counter—
those were real.

I keep living there.
Foolish. I am home. Half safe.

from

HEROES, ADVISE US   (1964)

Muscles and dogs.
    He made the endeavor,
   Took one step,
     And went on forever.

II   THE JOURNEY OUT

They left their base and October behind them,
the flag of empire curled on their sledges,
lured by the world's end, the southern tiptoe,
hub where all spokes of the turning map
plunged to a dot they could be first to conquer:
twelve men, eight ponies, the Russian dogs
running and tumbling, the ponies' manes lifting
like little trees. Horses hated the wind,
foraged for shelter, bucked at the death-smell
from a far glacier where they would be freed
of loads forever, their bullet-smoked haunches
sorted and eaten; ribs, hearts, liver
stored in a cairn flying the black flag
of a darker nation.

Oates
        Oates, the dragoon, the Iniskillin lover
of horseflesh and crystal and argent adventure,
tobacco-chewer, slogger, judge of stallions,
wrestled cold manes, fussed with fodder,
oil cakes, bran, built barns out of blizzards,
coaxed the pale hoofs of conquest closer,
heard the mare's whinny on the wind,
stroked a muzzle with pity in his palm,
said their names over and tried to forget them—
Jehu and Nobby, Chinaman, Snatcher—
chewed his pity and coughed it out
to make a brown flower in a white stable.

Tractors led the way, mechanical hope
riding on rollers, engines shuddering
in the hot cold that fired blizzards

into white sparks. Marchers, trapped
on blowing pavements, cheered the machines
they had not believed in, and their leader
hoped in spite of not hoping
while his great toys groaned across the Barrier
and the white road was blotched
with their black drippings
for a day, two days, five days, seven . . .

The throttle froze to the engineer's fingers
and his breath stroked like another engine,
knowing the metal veins could burst
and the rollers break like ice
on his forehead, but driving, driving
into the waste.
                  Cylinders split
in the crush of cold and the dark snouts rolled
into their graves without a whinny,
black ribs, black spines, dead spark and throttle
left to the jaws of a thousand winters.

Tracks of ponies, dogs, man-haulers
made a blue wreath of footsteps around them,
going on toward the Beardmore ice and the summit
and the bullets waiting for Chinaman and Jehu.
All could not last until the glacier
and these were the crocks, the weakening members.

        Jehu went first
        made four feedings
        for the dogs which must run
        their longer journey.

        Chinaman walked
        to the brink of December.

        The rest limped on
        with their manes blowing,
        only four bags
        of fodder among them

and seventy miles
to the end of their haul—
hundreds more for men—
and the land showing peaks
through the window of distance.
The window broke
and the tents trembled
like the green skin
of pointed beasts,
while only time marched
toward any conquest.

Four days and four nights
and ribs showing.

>   *One must stick it out*
>   *and hope for the best.*
>   *In a brief spell of hope*
>   *last night*
>   *one heard laughter.*

But rations must be stolen
from the future
for the howl of wind
was the howl of hunger
in spite of red, sweet
bones and haunches—
Christopher, Michael—
food for dogs
and English heroes.

>   *It is evil to lie here . . .*
>   *watching the mottled*
>   *wet green walls of our tent,*
>   *the glistening wet bamboos,*
>   *the bedraggled sopping socks . . .*
>   *to hear the falling snow*
>   *and the ceaseless rattle*
>   *of fluttering canvas . . .*
>   *to feel the wet clinging dampness*

of everything touched.
Add the stress of sighted failure
of our whole plan . . .
But, yet, after all,
one can go on striving . . .

Wilson

Sleeping bags were wet, but Wilson drew
the dry profile of a penguin in his diary,
the lean hand dreaming of rookeries
he had not reached through a hell of trying;
doctor, scholar, "tough as steel in the traces,"
although he had lived through thirty-nine winters
(but no summer like this)
with a spirit designed to burn through drifts
or hack a cliff down for the sake of a glint
of an unknown mica, metal, fossil.
Birds' eggs had beauty, and the aurora
streaming like the hair of a tall mermaid.
He sketched them, carried their brittle portraits
among the flags and food, and the opium
saved for some moment of decision,
while his pockets creaked
with stone discoveries.
One could never be weighed down
by the granite of knowledge,
and snow-blind eyes could see the glory
of conquest and science standing together
where he and Scotty would stand and unfold
the Union Jack on the turning axis.

They marched again,
the last march for ponies.
One pony endured
on a feast of biscuits
a lean hand spared
from its gaunt, day's ration.

Men, said the doctor
to his windy stomach,

could endure hunger
better than horses,
and watched Nobby canter
on stilts like legs—
and dreaded the bullet
that life required.

Bowers

At the beginning he was never cold,
wore his earlaps up, sweated in storms,
burned a wick that kept him going
like a furious elf swatting the knees
of something intolerable in the way.
"Birdie," they called when a thing needed seeing
or just seeing through. His eyes were small;
his nose would have hampered a larger man,
but he focused over a thousand miles
to the cold prize, saw the giant overthrown
and huddled beneath his straddling thighs.

He was the youngest of the five,
lieutenant, marine, captain of stores,
guardian of chocolate, pemmican, tea
and caches left for gnawing hands;
helper, hauler, contemptuous of sleep,
builder of trees out of paper and sticks
for Christmas in June—the branches gleamed
above a castle of foolish gifts,
whistles and popguns; handler of silk
where weather balloons like the wobbling heads
of strange, drowsy children
nodded against the birdless wind;
photographer, too, who found his lens
turned on a wizened, withering thing,
the Norwegian's banner clapping behind.
He trudged on legs as short as thumbs,
though lengthening to match his eyes,
and traveled farther than he knew.

The wind rises and falls . . .
We are struggling on,
considering all things,
against the odds.

    Ponies were dead, the dogs sent back.
      He led his eleven up a road
      Of buried glass where the glacier flowed
    Like an old man's beard, mourned the lack

    Of reasonable weather, and envied such ice
      As Shackleton found, blue under foot,
      Silk for sledges; scribbled a note
    To those in the vise

    Of a rear-guard camp, "I never felt fitter,"
      Took time to brag, "I kept up with the rest."
      But things were not rosy. The test
    Remained and the going was bitter.

    He did his sums, measured his men,
      Subtracted three for the last run,
      Saw Bowers' eyes and added one
    In spite of the plan, went on again,

    Shaping farewell to the other seven—
      Good fellows all, but all could not go.
      Through green goggles he watched the snow
    Fall like a city, and fought for vision.

Evans
    This was the strong man, fixer of sledges,
    six feet tall, two-hundred pound mast
    for hope to lean on. A royal seaman,
    he learned to ride an unruled ocean
    beyond one empire to another, but found
    strength could plunge like a falling anchor
    through the steep foam of shoreless blizzards.
    His brain was a cupboard hoarding details
    of crampons, ski shoes, each thread and tool
    that made the machinery of triumph

more supple; corrected faults of harness
and will but could not mend a deepening fault
that traveled with him, felt himself dwindle,
supporting a giant whose open mouth,
crammed with wind, swallowed whole dreams
of beef and mutton.
                    Rations were equal
for equal courage. Honor demanded
the hoosh be measured, biscuits divided
between lean and stalwart. He asked nothing more,
but his long bones ranted, clattered like teeth,
down the thinning miles.

    1

Huge, uninhabited, roughly circular,
highest of the continents, windiest, coldest,
hardest to reach, perpetually hostile,
pivot where the polar anticyclone snarls
seaward from the sepulchres of upheaved mountains.

In five million square miles no walking beast
leaves the blue stamp of paw or hoof,
and only wind, or the southern lights
singing like rayon, charges the silence.
Voices are unknown except for those of pilgrims
climbing the bleak, ascending forehead
of a plateau that ends in constellations
where the true cross shines like a golden raft,
guide of mariners on a midnight ocean.
Larger and lower, the false crucifix
lures the unwary, and betrays.

Only the rootless snow makes meadows,
yet glaciers hold in their gray coffins
dead spines of fern, the fossil lace
of sequoia leaves, while Mount Erebus,
large as a nation,
blows fire from his spuming lip
like sparks of nameless, falling birds.

Some tropic memory haunts the wind
and neither men nor mountains know
what root is straining underfoot,
what branches are reaching overhead.

>   *I had pinned my faith*
>   *on better conditions . . .*
>   *We can but toil on . . .*

far from England,
snow melting into walls
around their knees,
crossbars trapped
in the sweating drifts,
two-hundred pound sledges
moving, barely,
reaching two thousand feet
and fog,
and sly crevases,
blue lips in the beard.
Men went down to the length of a harness,
like breaking through a glass house . . .
As first man, I get first chance.
It's exciting not knowing
which step will give way.

Camp forty-six, altitude eight thousand.
>   *The wind is continuous from the south-southeast,*
>   *very searching . . .*
>   *and about us is a scene of the wildest desolation,*
>   *but we are a very cheerful party*
>   *and tomorrow is Christmas Day . . .*

Night camp fifty-one, height nine thousand.
>   *There have been some hours of very steady plodding . . .*
>   *these are the best part of the business,*
>   *they mean forgetfulness and advance.*

Night camp fifty-four. Fourteen below.
>   *A stick of chocolate to celebrate the New Year.*

Camp fifty-six. The summit of farewell
for the five going on and the returning party,
only one hundred and forty-six miles
between them now and the white magnet.

The captain hated his role, dreaded the hurt
of those not chosen for the last hazard.
One man wept. The others pulled masks
over their faces, shook hands and turned,
and one remembered for forty years after
the diminishing specks, five dots on a scroll
of illimitable gray, the tall wind behind,
and the horizon curling upward and over.

Camp fifty-eight. Twenty-three below.
> *We sigh for a breeze to sweep the hard snow.*
> *We go little over a mile and a quarter an hour now . . .*
> *it is a big strain as the shadows creep slowly round*
> *from our right through ahead to our left.*
> *What lots of things we think of . . .*
> *What castles one builds now hopefully that the Pole is ours.*

Under the ice was a deeper danger
  his mind skidded on. He pulled fear tight,
braced it with pride. He was no sprinter.
  Science was the rock. But still the white,
loping sun held the shadow
  of that other figure which had started before him.
Nights in a night-assaulted tent
  he found his dreams stapled to the rim
of a yapping void, saw Amundsen's dogs
  with flapping tongues gallop past
his lame ponies, woke with sweat
  caught in his hands, glimpsed a vast
landscape of teeth on end, turned to his letters,
  trusting in language to deliver a meaning
beyond disaster. *It's the work that counts,*
  not the applause that follows. The wild, leaning
canvas became a sky flung across cricket fields and ships.
  Racing was not what one went out for,

but hope reared on legs as hard as the whips
   rapped over a shuddering spine of huskies
his dread sent toward the revolving shrine
    hung between antipodal seas, the blended oceans,
      and the hard whine
      of continuing silence,
      continuing marches—
      camp sixty-one,
      sixty-two,
      sixty-five,
and the killer at the center, waiting.

> *All is new ahead . . .*
> *Our chance still holds . . .*
> *We have covered six miles*
> *but at fearful cost . . .*
>
> *Another hard grind*
> *and five miles added . . .*
> *All the time the sledge*
> *rasps and creaks.*
> *We ought to get through . . .*
> *but, oh! for a better surface . . .*
> *So close it seems*
> *and only the weather to baulk us.*

Only the weather and fatigue and hunger
and the cold cutting deeper in spite of sunlight.
Oates, slogging on through whinnying silence,
fancied at times he heard the brittle
step of a pony just behind him
and felt a red ghost nuzzle his shoulder.
Evans chewed the wind, tried not to remember
the taste of things glowing in ovens
or sprouting green out of a garden.
The sky was warmer, the drifts softened,
but cold had become an interior host
dressed and marching in their bodies.
Even Bowers, the "little marvel," felt the chill
drive through some invisible doorway

to reach the fire under his ribs
though the fire in his legs still blazed,
while Wilson, leaning against the traces,
considered the medicines in his bag
and found no antidote but marching
another mile, three miles, four,
heard Scott breathing hard beside him.
The breath seemed his own. He had written,
"There is nothing I would not do for him,"
rewrote it now on the smoking air,
stumbled, straightened, made another mile,
grateful to be there, glad to be chosen.

2

This is the land of superior mirages,
distortions, dreams, repeated rainbows,
false sunsets and deceptive sunrises,
ships overturned yet serenely riding
the high abyss as if to some anchor
hung between Polaris and the Goat.

The wisest visitors have been misled,
followed the wrong image, found themselves
trapped in a hall of carnival mirrors
where the glassy air's inverted lens
reflects an insupportable landscape,
makes grotesque the simplest being,
and holds the golden oasis forever
one inch away from the scheming hand.

Even at the gate where the first floes drift
like dead messengers from some wrinkled tomb,
the *fata morgana* magnifies and lifts
the wind's debris into steeples,
hoists cathedrals against the sky,
erects such cities, a pilgrim imagines
Atlantis risen with all its green towers,
garlands, and women, and stalks through the crystal
into the darkness behind every mirror.

Early explorers followed a mirage
twisting with angels and horny fires,
recorded phantoms as veritable flesh,
pursued illusion beyond the round edge
of experience and the orbiting world,
believed the wind was turned by a fist
so faceted, jeweled, encumbered with light,
mortals must be blinded by a glimpse
of one radiant knuckle. Other voyagers,
the cold still creaking in their hair,
reported an unimaginable forehead,
eyeless, Neanderthal, sloping into heaven
from the loud jaws of a gaping sea.

Some circumnavigating this circle
flee what they find, leave it for saints
or merchants to conquer, retire to rest homes,
diseases, games. Others go through
to that crevasse where the last mirror hands
and the staring self dangles in its worn harness
over a void, while breath crashes
like a blue, falling window.

Only the mirage lives through these winters,
and the boneless wind sniffing at tracks
fixed like a wreath where the most recent traveler
has pitched his blind, enduring tent.

>   *Bright southerly wind . . . low drift . . .*
>   *I could see nothing . . .*
>   *Bowers on my shoulders directed me . . .*
>   *two long marches would land us at the Pole.*
>   *. . . the only appalling possibility*
>   *the sight of the Norwegian flag*
>   *forestalling ours.*

Bowers' eyes were too keen,
saw almost too clearly
from his breathing roost

the unnatural shrine
at the sky's taut edge.

He felt uneasy,
tried to believe
he glimpsed only a shadow
the fumbling wind
had dropped like a cloth.

The speck seemed no larger
than the grave of a fly,
then lunged at sight,
sang like a hook,
dragged him nearer
until he envisioned
some tireless angler
turning a reel
where miles were wound
like rasping silk,
and looked through lashes
suddenly haloed
at the flag, sledge bearer,
tracks of dogs and men,
remains of a camp,
unremaining illusion.

3

It stood there pitched beyond revision,
its bamboo steeple supporting the blue,
white-bordered cross on a crimson field,
simple, deadly, compact, in order—
the other man's tent, the other king's banner,
poised at the creaking end of a journey
where orderly hope, orderly motion
became disorder for all explorers
who start too late, find the wrong weather,
misjudge the hour or the risk of arrival.

It is always too late, too huge, too little,
the island ruined, the city taken,
and we keep arriving at the place
we thought we had left safely behind us,
find the same face in the bedroom closet,
familiar dust in secret corners,
the litter staring from under the rug,
or simply the failure at the world's end
when what is attained is another journey
longer than the first and with less expectation.

The captain made his account, kept language trim,
    recorded weather, dodged despair.
Twenty-two below and a nagging chill.
    The pole was there, but no longer theirs.
His pencil bucked, paused at the edge—
    "All the day dreams must go"—
stumbled on pity. "I am very sorry
    for my loyal companions." He heard the snow,
white leaves descending over a tent
    they might never leave, felt fear
joggle his elbow. "The wind is blowing hard."
    It was nothing new. All was old here;
the trail ahead, the trail back;
    the trail back, the trail ahead,
and the future mired in the past.
    Only the chill was deeper, and dread.
Latitude eighty-nine. Drifting tracks.
    Tomorrow the wind might be a friend.
Stiff upper lip. Courage. Duty.
    Face the run home. Ascend, descend
but keep on slogging—Something whined and shuddered,
    invisible, huge, carrying the wind
on its own haunches, crept to his feet,
    fawned there, suffered; yet, suffering, grinned . . .
He half-nodded, dreaming, remembered too late
    It's the work that counts—could not erase
"Great God!" where his leaping pencil charged
    an indelible page ". . . this is an awful place

and terrible enough for us to have laboured to it
    without the reward of priority."
The race had been real, though the goal was false.
    He turned his back, drank English tea,
considered the eight hundred miles ahead—
    behind—nowhere—the treacherous wind,
the smoking abyss, and measured the chance
of a green shore. It would be a near thing.

4

They stood at the mathematical point
where every direction is the same,
facing the camera's simple eye,
their own eyes blinded by a sun
that never moved, late visitors with little time
to brood on fashion or design;
still wore their sweat-stained harnesses,
shivered in baggy uniforms,
let their mittened hands droop at their sides,
furred and heavy, like severed paws.

There were no smiles, although one tried,
or seemed to try. Images blur across the miles
it takes to reach a multi-colored wheel
where drugstore paperbacks display
heroes more common to the age,
ruddier, swifter, less inclined
to risk illusion or despair.

Gray faces, gray flags. Colors were there—
though limited—the wind-charred ear,
the hidden wound growing like a jewel
on a silver heel, a blackening nail,
the violet, bone-centered chill.

They posed, exposed to the rough stare
of something beyond the winking lens—
death's head, or hope, or just our gaze
slanted across a feverish aisle

of tranquilizers, lotions, toys,
where we, like them, look past the void
to practice an imperfect smile.

III   THE JOURNEY BACK

They marched with the wind,
a south breeze behind them,
hoisted a sail
to the plunging sled,
watched it billow,
an earthly ship riding
the dreaded snow waves
of crooked sastrugi.
Runners stuck fast
where crystal showers
turned drifts to sand,
covered their tracks
as if only ghosts
were laboring onward.

It was everything now
to keep a good pace,
reach the depots
where food was cached—
Half Degree, Half Ton,
Three Degree, Summit,
Desolation, Shambles
(dead ponies waiting)—
fifty miles, ninety,
a hundred, three hundred,
thousands, a million . . .
Mathematics failed.
All miles were multiplied by hunger
and the faltering pace
of dragoon and giant,
the rusting links,
weakening members.

Wilson and Bowers are my standby.
But he stood alone, night on his forehead,
searching for error, some miscalculation.
(As a child he had been lazy,
too much the dreamer, given to tantrums,
was called "Old Moony.") He had fought back,
corrected nature. This nature was different,
and not his doing. All was risk.
That was what they had come for!
And the plan was true. No man could manage
fate or weather, or offer insurance
against chagrin. (One must preserve
a sense of proportion.)
Yet he may have missed the telling thing:
monotony, boredom, the featureless city
set beyond gardens or Monday's wash,
mailmen, the treble voice of children . . .

No, the error was failure.
Dogs might have been surer,
chops and cutlets
on the brightening snow,
but his design called for men
hauling their shadows
into a shadow. Amundsen won,
had never been moony,
knew that a whip could extend a horizon.
His mind closed, hot as a visor.

Evans' nose was frostbitten.
Oates had a cold foot.
Fifty-five miles;
four days of food.
The plan had been right,
all risks considered, but . . .
A long way to go . . .
we are pretty thin . . .
and, by Jove,
this is tremendous labour.

The chance still held,
in spite of blizzards
or the sail hanging slack
like a dirty wrinkle.
Hope ran ahead
with a good day's slogging.

Excellent march. Wind helping greatly.
It is all soft and sandy beneath the glaze.
Thank God, the miles are coming fast.
This is the bright side.
The reverse of the medal is serious.
Wilson has strained a tendon—
of course, he is full of pluck.
Evans has dislodged two fingernails . . .

They reached into February,
twenty-seven days from the pole,
had the summit's rock underfoot again,
felt like sailors reaching land,
stroked the dark foreheads of granite and quartz,
staggered toward knowledge,
the only prize left.
Empty stomachs could wait
while empty hands clutched
something for science.

Thirty pounds of specimen rock
was heaped on the sled that hunger must pull,
and Wilson, searching through snow-burned eyes,
found a ghost of greenery
in a black seam, memory of a leaf
throbbing on coal; imagined it growing
into branches of lilac, boxwood, laurel,
traced a numb finger along the traces
of what had been living. Blown snow rustled
like a tree, and the wind felt warmer—
while the Beardmore waited with its crevasses.

They had known the blue-gray gullets before,
vertical throats of an albino herd
buried to the eyes in basements of snow,
but direction had changed. They veered toward a trap,
teetered on chasms, found themselves blocked
by ribs of chaos, hacked a way through
but lost the day, depleted reserves,
stretched three pemmican meals to four,
prayed that the wind, and strength, would hold,
though Evans' strength had already broken.
Only a giant will, or dread, moved the giant
across the landscape. A blistered heel dragged
an extra furrow between the sledge's double track,
and Wilson and Bowers, the standbys, were blind
from the blind sun, and the effort of vision.

　　Breakfast tea and one gray biscuit.
　　The Cloudmaker ahead. Every drift held a flag
　　of a phantom depot. Evans cried out,
　　lured by a shadow. Yet a depot was there
　　and the speck of food that would keep them marching
　　toward a chimera—rain-winnowed evenings
　　beside a fire, a clean table sagging
　　with hills of mutton, veal, roast, pheasant,
　　jellies, puddings, buckets of gravy . . .

　　　　We have reduced food; also sleep.
　　　　A rather trying position.
　　　　Evans has nearly broken down in brain . . .

but under the skull-surrounded mind,
the fractured will pursued a pattern:
limp on, stagger, dodge the crevasse,
remember the goal, hunt for more flags,
depots, caches, something to gnaw on,
knuckles of wind, haunch of the blizzard.
Six-foot pigmy. Fixer of sledges,
loser of nails. For lack of a nail . . .
The pattern splintered. Snow turned to a tide,
swallowed his ankles, foamed toward his thighs.

He lagged behind, swimming through marble.
They turned and waited, hauled with their voices,
made a net of smiles. He begged for a string—
excuse to linger, ruse to tie a chasm together,
lace up the void; felt the tide gather
and darkness stampede out of a cavern
that seemed within him, tore off his mittens.
The wind was on fire. He scorched his hands
in the freezing sky—tugged at his clothing—
watched his captors turn, returning,
the blind leading the blind. Only he saw clearly,
though the look was wild; and, seeing, surrendered.

> *He died a natural death,*
> *and we did not leave him*
> *until two hours after . . .*

Four going on. Score One for the land.
Score Two ticking as they watched the "Soldier,"
Titus Oates, pride of the dragoons,
wade through time on swelling ankles.

Shambles Camp and a resurrection—
Snatcher, Nobby, Bones, Michael—
dead steeds that a limping rider might spur
out of congealing dust to glory,
if feet like his could reach a stirrup.

> *I wonder what is in store for us,*
> *with some little alarm*
> *for the lateness of the season.*

An old saw makes a marching rhythm.
   It is always later than you think,
And growing later, growing colder.
   A watch betrays and summers slink

Toward early winters. The final march
   Is always near, though you may think

yet plateaus are black with men marching
   toward an end they cannot measure.

These, at this pole, were decimals
   set within an infinite figure;
staggered through the multiple cold
   to reach the indivisible cipher.

Monday:
   Regret to say, going from bad to worse.
   No time for literary ornament now,
   nor concern for the vanished auroral lights
   that had nicked his lines with poetry
   at a vanished camp. He had seen, in those skies,
   ghosts leaning behind the ghostly gleams:
   invisible neighbors in other worlds
   sending their signals through the dark,
   symbols and glowing signatures,
   and had yearned for a key, thought it strange
   men had not knelt and worshipped such splendor.

   Now sky had become nothing but weather,
   a lunatic mouth babbling of cold,
   and only the wind left a signature
   scribbled on snow, or set like a brand
   of a white herdsman on cheek and forehead,
   indecipherable, beyond translation.
   The only communicant was his hand
   moving by inches on a brittle page.
   Some message might blaze, like those ancient lights,
   across time's great and wrinkled furrow
   to send, through space, its spangled cry
   for men to decipher into meaning.

      Got a slant of wind yesterday afternoon.
      Converted our wretched morning run
      of three-and-a-half to something over nine.
      Started the march on tea and pemmican,
      solid with the chill off.
      We pretend to prefer it that way.

Fuel dreadfully low;
the poor Soldier nearly done.
He makes no complaint,
but he grows more silent.

All lights seemed low.

Tuesday:
*We mean to see the game through
with a proper spirit.*

Wednesday:
*A little worse I fear.
We still talk of what we will do together at home.*

Thursday:
*Worse and worse in morning . . .
Oates' left foot can never last out . . . ·
Wilson's feet giving trouble now,
but this is mainly because
he gives so much help to the others . . .*

Thirty pounds of rock
still rode the sledge.
Rock of ages.
Something for science.

Friday:
No entry.

Saturday:
*Things steadily downhill.
Oates' foot worse.
He has rare pluck
and must know that he can never get through.*

Knowing is not the same as believing;
belief is not the same as knowing.
A little more food, a sweeter wind,
and who knows what morning will bring?

The chance may hold, the doctor says.
But he may be lying. And God knows what
is written down in the brown diary.

Oates is a hindrance? Oates dooms us all?
Oates must march or we cannot march?
Oates is dying? Oates is brave?

He is wonderfully brave.
He is a brave fine fellow.
Titus Oates is very near the end.
Oates is silent, knowing, enduring.
The poor Soldier has become a terrible hindrance,
though he does his utmost
and suffers much, I fear.

Suffering could end. Scott gave the order,
made Wilson unlock the crucial packet
where opium hid, thirty tabloids apiece,
with a tube of morphine left for the doctor.
Rations had always been equally shared.
No man could protest that he had been cheated—
yet death would be cheated and one's honor.

Each man drew his harness over his shoulders,
limped on, contemptuous of the bitter mercy
stored in a pocket, looked half-guilty
for the reserve filched from a deeper larder,
and carried courage like a secret
until he saw on each bruised face
the same proud guilt, the equal measure.

Oates stumbled on through four more days,
then asked to be left in his sleeping bag.
No one would leave. He must blunder on,
hauling his senseless feet beyond
horizons of sense—one step, another,
three and five, counting, falling,
lagging in time like a crippled clock;
hindrance, horror, pain's old companion.

He steered toward one more camp and slept,
prayed that he would not wake, but woke,
sloughed off his cocoon, heard the blizzard
cry like a mare, white mane blowing,
imagined silver reins in his fingers,
stood up in a shapeless uniform,
spurs missing, boots unpolished.
"I'm just going outside
and may be some time."

> They waited, knowing
> they waited for no one,
> counted each other
> in the rocking minutes.
> Three for the sledge.
> Three still marching.

> *We all hope to meet the end*
> *with a similar spirit,*
> *and assuredly the end is not far.*

Friday or Saturday:
  Lost track of dates.
  But minus forty. Minus hope.
  Number Fourteen Camp.
  Only two pony marches away
  from One Ton Depot.
  One more chance.

Sunday, March 18:
  Ill fortune presses,
  but better may come.
  My right foot has gone,
  nearly all the toes . . .
  Amputation is the least
  I can hope for now.
  And the most.

> Would the knife hurt
> if it came to cutting?

He remembered Evans,
the giant treasure,
remembered Oates,
tender with ponies,
both of them under
the white road and whitening;
saw Bowers' live eyes,
the "undefeated little sportsman,"
watched Wilson contrive
the wisp of a smile,
"the best of comrades,
staunchest of friends,"
and heard, outside,
new blizzards arriving,
clung to his pencil,
tried to remember
the day and hour
or what should be written
to those going on
in other countries:
wives, mothers, sisters,
the special friends . . .
felt the pencil stiffen.

The end was not far,
but one must reach the end,
address each letter,
reassure, comfort,
explain to the public
there had been no error,
only risks misjudged,
adventure undertaken
to the last gasp of the threshing wind;
leviathan, angel, hooked and gaffed,
the stiff wings spearing upended mountains,
flukes, white with frost, scraping a tent
of shuddering cloth, and eyes rolling.

The land itself was a whirling sky,
and the whirling sky became the land

where every definition stopped;
dragoon and doctor, pigmy, giant,
and the man who led, dissolved
and absolved in the centrifuge
that spins the world.

To Mrs. E. A. Wilson:
  If this letter reaches you
  Bill and I will have gone out together.
  We are very near it now
  and I should like you to know
  how splendid he was . . .
  His eyes have a comfortable blue look of hope . . .

To Mrs. Bowers:
  As troubles have thickened,
  his dauntless spirit ever shone brighter . . .
  The ways of Providence are inscrutable,
  but there must be some reason why such a young,
  vigorous and promising life is taken . . .
  My whole heart goes out to you in pity.

To Sir J. M. Barrie:
  We are pegging out in a very comfortless spot.
  I am not at all afraid of the end,
  but sad to miss many a humble pleasure
  which I had planned for the future
  on our long marches . . .

To his wife:
  Make the boy a strenuous man.
  I had to force myself into being strenuous, as you know—
  had always an inclination to be idle.

  What lots and lots I could tell you of this journey.
  How much better has it been
  than lounging in too great comfort at home.

      He had four days to write,
      four days of blizzard

that reared between them
and the One Ton goals;
eleven miles only,
but a continuous gale
from the south, southwest.
Two cups of tea.
Two crumbs of food.

Eleven miles only,
eleven years,
time blowing in
like a sky of needles,
all things whirled
into disaster.

> For my own sake
> I do not regret this journey.

Perhaps they dozed,
perhaps they dreamed,
each in a sack
designed for rest
but not for a continuous slumber.
Was it Bowers or Wilson
who slept first and forever?
while Scott stayed awake
with his awful dream,
flung his hand over
the absent Wilson,
ordered his trifles—
scraps of flags,
the black flag and the other—
finished his permanent messages
to countrymen, widows,
and the admiralty.

The end is not known,
but it was never far,
as these three knew
when they pitched their house

of blowing fabric,
made it tidy
(order was a quality
apart from weathers)
made it taut,
made it secure,
the door facing down
the sharp sastrugi,
bamboos placed with a good spread,
and guarded against snow
in the inner lining.

Someone made a lamp wick
from the little fringe
of a tattered boot.
He may have written by that
or by some other wick
dipped in a spirit
jealously hoarded
against the last light.

There was surely darkness
beyond the white blizzard
and hands reaching to hands
across the crevasse
that widened, steepened,
plunged into glass,
stained windows, steeples,
churches of memory,
Christ with his lambs,
the noisy prophets,
and the world falling
but never failing
for the marchers, believers,
perdurable seekers
of the next mile, the inch,
the elaborate crystal
snow makes in falling,
eternal design of crucifix, frond,
star and odd angel.

He apologized, pitied,
put language away
and accepted the summons.

> *It seems a pity*
> *but I do not think I can write more.*

IV

Magellan mistook Tierra del Fuego
for the northern coast.
Drake did not like what he saw,
judged by the sample
that the hidden bulk
was not worth discovery,
looked sourly on landscapes condemned
to everlasting rigidity by Nature,
left it for resolute fools to conquer.

Merchant-adventurers sniffed the wind,
heard sirens bark from rookeries,
sailed their ships farther into shoals
where icebergs glided, large as churches
packed with gargoyles.
Islands turned red, but Weddell combined
blood with science, stuffed a seal,
gave it his name, and named a sea.
French, English, Russians, Americans
caulked their portholes against the cold,
steered toward the southern sepulchre,
recalling tales of a fertile land
hooked to the bottom of the world,
found penguins, scurvy, a million birds,
and the lucrative whale, blue as a fountain.

Some went farther, tried for the center
beyond experience or profit,
staggered back but kept on searching:
Biscoe, Balleny, Ross, Wilkes,

D'Urville, Mawson, Reynolds, Scott,
Shackleton, Amundsen, and Scott once more,
Scott forever, a part of the center,
integral, heaped there, the land's new bounty.

Its name is borrowed from the Greek,
anti (opposite) and *arktos* (bear),
that glowing mammal with the North Star
hitched to his unwavering tail.

No one knows how it began, laboring and lifting
its folded mountains, massifs, cliffs.
The sea's rough corridors were tipped
beneath some crude Pacific thrust,
and sediments soared into peaks
enclosing starfish and strange fern
whose tiny backbones sweat in rock.

Loud forests grew, when Africa was ice,
and, maybe, roses, untutored birds
with voices strained though musical.

And, it may be, trees will come again,
or glaciers turn to waterfalls
blowing like clouds, or the windy seeds
and spores of plants drift in to stamp
green hoofs upon the riderless hills,
and a skeleton wake with Lazarus eyes,
or eyes of dead explorers caught
in an iron sheath, eleven strides away
from the last cairn.
                        A leaf could crash,
yellow as thunder, or one root try
its lengthening nerve on the cloth of tombs,
pry open the tucked and pleated tents
of gathered mountains, until the whole, unlashed skull
blooms like a round and buzzing flower.

The epoch lingers and the dead stay dead,
though nothing in these latitudes can perish.

Decay is unknown, whether of flesh or language.
Hands that clasped once are forever clasped,
and love preserved is forever risen,
while the unchanging eyes, strict as jewels,
stare through a rent in the woven sky
at a sky beyond, centered on visions
we cannot cancel nor revise.

> *After all, one can go on striving.*
> *In a brief spell of hope last night*
> *one heard laughter.*

Ice Age

Often, in summer, I forget those heroes
who with white beards invaded the future
where icebergs swam like birds on water,
cold beaks turned to a ship's slaughter.

I forget, under oaks, the lack of flowers
and the tenor of dogs that must be eaten,
their bones bluer than the mouths of heroes.
But in certain dreams the fissure narrows

between cut stars and my heavy lilies
and shapes my pillow into a drift.
The future skates into my marrow.
A cap slides askew. Heroes, advise us.

Achilles

My heel always ached a little,
    as if the beak of a pin
sang there, and sometimes a nerve
    jumped like a candle. But in
those hot years when we fought
    for beauty—in ways
that made deeper wounds
    than nature gave us—the blaze
of hope seemed immortal armor.
    There were such stars then,
swimming in our shields,
    and gods blowing through men
as through locusts. Motion
    of boughs in a night wind was more
than eyes looked for; angels
    attended our wars, and the roar
of wind through our tents
    was the crimson baying of
our certain hearts. I have seen cattle
    as bright as roses, and doves
making a white ocean of a cliff
    of lilacs. But that was before
the arrow found me, small and tidy
    as a recent tooth—inquisitor,
spy—that worked like a key there,
    unfastened bad dreams,
infected the sea wind and the lost air,
    drove to extremes
the mortal desire
    to be immortal again,
until I leaped, my own arrow,
    at the perfect pain
of that wedge buried
    in the exposed cup
my mother missed in her prayers
    and ablution. They were not enough.

I should have gone armed
       with iron boots to my armpits,
for my heel aches now
       like a lark on a spit,
and the urn where I turn
       is a tower of myth
turned by sea scum
       and the wind's black breath.

Plaza de Toros, Iowa

The cornhusk mattress creaks
like an empty church;
my grandfather in sleep
hunts for his death, a toreador
caught in a noise of crows and cocks.
A cat with eyes of a doll
watches from under my chair,
watching the dust that creeps.
A curtain blows like a cape.
Something whisks past,
darker than water,
louder than a leaf.

The wind is round in his porcelain mouth
where his hard breath knocks
and the bony crescents clack
like hoofs of a running horse.
The last snore comes through a canter of teeth.

The bed is still. The window shines.
Rats in the woodshed leave their chores.
The roosters cease.
A bull that panted all night long
holds his black breath
and I see his horns blue-white and cold
like the parentheses of a lyre.

The Allergic

An angel at the door can make them sneeze
or blue light breaking from a miller's wing,
so nice is the disorder of their breath,
so windswept is the heart of everything.

Gazelles must keep in bounds, and orioles
transport their gold combines to darker trees;
the world of pelt and plume and naked rose
is battered by the dust's duplicities.

The rain brings succor, but the rain is brief;
behind it, like a horse, the black wind rears
and gallops to their nostrils. Pity these
who when they weep must weep with dusty tears.

Mote

The hummingbird, acquaintance,
hanging at the feeder,
fencing with his beak,
suspended as by whirling arms
or two round harps,
is instant color.

Here we have a minute thunder,
mandolin, banjo, fever,
potential crisis of motion
as in a spinning jenny
grown eccentric, its cotton raveling
into a knot like a flower.

This spinner ends in rainbow,
and so begins.
(The inside of the egg, surely,
is a centrifuge of opals.)

He rests, rarely and neatly,
after his spike explores
honey trapped in glass and jasmine.
He goes to that rest so swiftly
he is nearly a myth. He becomes
a bud on a twig of a bough.
He dives into wind as into water.
He lifts himself, or is lifted,
into a feathered diamond
greener than the leaves
he brings his light to.

He is an uncertain visitor,
unpredictable, fickle, late to appointments,
obsessed with nectar in distant cabinets.

But when he comes, shining the window,
and leans there, gleams in his cape,
tips his javelin and remains,
we lay down our books, music, cards,
and watch like the cats
who are also our boarders,
as helpless as they
to stay that mote by talons or love.

Affinities

Dusk is in the cat.
It stores its shadow
in the black loft of his bones
where his ribs hang
from the spine rod.
Thunder's loose guitar
is in him,
in miniature,
and the thistle's fire.
The world is sharper
for the shape of his ears
and the blue wishbones of sparrows.

Mirages

... the surviving horse, driven frantic by thirst, thrust his mouth
into the flames of a campfire under the illusion that it was water.
                                          World of the Desert—Ernest

Pegasus found shelter in the heavenly stalls of Olympus . . .
                                          Mythology—Hamilton

. . . How the sand came at us, color of Corinth
and broken cornstalks,
how the wind burst its bag of clouds,
how we sought an oasis as green as Iowa,
how the camels stank and at night chewed their cuds,
how by day their legs rowed like leather oars
through the hot, blowing sea,
and their eyes shone as through brown water
while the impatient horses (brittle possessions
the nomads say, but good for war)
were forever hungry, thirsty, or dancing,
whinnying around the coffee fires
and the tents pitched like motionless waves.

. . . How I groomed one horse (one I brought with me
out of harness and the shadow of silos,
though he had drunk at the hippocrene spring),
rubbed him as bright as a birch in sleet . . .
how I fed him herbs so crisp they chirped
between his teeth, and the milk of camels,
bringing it in bowls, the warm foam frothing
whiter than his blizzard-thick, sun-scalded mane . . .
then escaped the herdsmen with shrewd rat faces,
and the women working at their shrill distaffs
(none was an explorer, none sought the horizon
with its blue harbors, chimeras, temples),
galloped off like a sail under billowing starlight.

64

. . . How we saw before us, just before dawn,
the five-fingered hand of the desert hare,
and thought, for an instant, we were saluted.

. . . How the sun thickened and the wind changed;
heat was a gong in a brass bell's throat,
lamenting, loud; how we passed the hedgehog,
the wolf, and vermin, and seed-hunting ants
heaped over with cargo; how the scorpion
lifted his pallid steeple; how the carrion eagle,
small but sudden, turned as we turned;
how the sun fell in ruins at every sunset,
and frost rose like needles;
how we licked the cold dew
and shivered together, heart to haunch,
yet dreading the furnace of the sun's resurrection—
and sought Olympus beyond the next morning.

. . . How we descended craters, ascended sandstone,
lost the compass in a drifting castle,
tripped on thorn trees and went on, pawing bronze spaces—
I in my armor, he in his bridle—
and how, near the end, I had to tug him,
how his white mane thawed,
how when we found water
(bones in it and shrapnel)
it crackled like fire
between his dry teeth . . .
how we were troubled with gnats and leeches—
dark wreaths for his eyes—
and how sky and sand became lava.

. . . How I searched for searchers, and how I listened
for a camel's cough or the whine of a distaff,
and yearned in my throat for dark rain or wine
or the locusts roasted for a stranger,
but fought back a surrender to these gods.

. . . How it was my steed who ended the journey
and threw me, returned to a plow horse,

acquired visions of commonest clover,
brayed with thirst like a saw, forget his wings,
sought for a pond in a plain farmer's pasture,
grew a wild eye that rolled like a marble.

. . . How when I kindled an evening fire
he mistook the flames for water,
plunged his mouth in and gulped the red fountain,
screamed like a wire, and leaped upward,
his nostrils streaming gray roses of smoke . . .
                              how I went, blinded, back
to the hair-cloth tents, the herdsmen and housewives,
the sound of the coffee pestle, the snores of old men,
the wells stained yellow from pollutions,
my beggar's bowl always extended.
. . . How I, like Bellerophon before me,
grope through the stalls of dust,
unmoved by hope or hoof or caravan
beneath the nickering sky.

Ghost

Dream is a darkness troubled by sisters,
mothers, a friend, the wraith of a fish
with a hook in both eyes, a pet dog dying
and resurrected like a Christ in fur,
and black umbrellas that refuse to open.

Last night I saw her, helped her to the table,
lied about pain, forced her to eat
out of my hunger. Tablespoons lay crooked
against the oilcloth, and my hand was an animal
trying to correct them.
"We'll put them straight tomorrow," I said,
but told another, "She'll be dead by then."
As she was, and is, with the spoons still crooked.

I believe in ghosts.
I lay awake, dreaming, looking at grass
in the living moonlight—and something chirred:
frog, cricket, bird. For a moment I thought
it was a voice that mattered.

Native Land

In that country the wind
in his howl jackhammers
hawks from their wheels,
and ice boards up the pickerel's comet
and staples the carp into his meadow,
and the runners of sleet
through the metal forest
buckle the rabbit's eyes to his eyelid.
In that country a wolf
with a tin face follows
the grooves of a doe,
her knees unfastened,
and a mouse staggers
under the cliff
of the raven's boiling shadow.

from

SHORT HISTORY OF THE FUR TRADE   (1968)

Short History of the Fur Trade

COSTUME BOOK (Excerpt One)

Lions were always high style,
the tail, a bearded rope,
glowing from angular pharaohs' belts;
the paws, chrysanthemums with thorns,
flung over priestly torsos
in a dead embrace.
Nero used the whole beast beneath his throne,
its mane spread out like a yellow ocean's wave,
head hollowed, scooped, and stuffed,
the fangs intent as jewels,
the eyes (the footstool's staring radiance)
trapped under sandals beating time
to a tin lyre and the gusty cries
from torches shaped like burning rows of men.

Queen Semiramis, heiress of Babylon,
was fond of tigers, marched to India
with a million spears, reeled back before the roar
of elephants that rose like wrinkled walls,
but carried home a thousand skins
whose brown and supple lightning bolts
hummed like doves beneath her lingering hand.

Leopards, too, were popular
with those who could afford such flowers
blossoming on wall or couch,
as when the Great Khan, hunting
with his barons, cooks, and hawks,
set up his pointed cities on the trail,
covering each sable-curtained tent
with gardens stitched from golden hides
on which the dark geranium leaves
rippled in wind as if alive.

The fox's brush was popular with kings,
flared on the tips of lances
like a bushy flame, while Chinese mandarins
and Vandal lords yawned into bed
beneath the silk-lined plush
of weasel, moleskin, any soft, denuded thing
the hunters peeled and left
to stare at heaven through its sudden skull.

The poor made do with common pelts—
rabbit and dog, the soft brocade of cats—
but dreamed beneath their calluses and lice
of a new world where ermine flowed
to every poacher's trap,
seeing around them (a brittle fleece
scattered on alp and steppe and moor)
only the comfortless, dead white
of drift on drift of deepening bones.

Monarchs, too, felt the swift cold,
began to keep the rarer beasts
(thought-furrowed apes, gazelles, and deer)
in fountain-plumed menageries;
sent huntsmen sniffing toward fresh seas,
found beaver hats and otter muffs,
brown, booming robes of buffalo,
the neat pronghorn, the narrow wolf,
and grizzlies rearing up like shaggy towers—
       and then again
    the drift on drift of bones.

        The zoo preserves some specimens,
        the penny-colored lion, the shopworn bear,
        and tigers lend a spark to circuses,
        while delicate foxes with trade names
        (Royal Pastel, Starlight, and Silver Blue)
        pant through a fur farm's lethal door
        toward breathless evenings on Nob Hill,
        and Easter morning on Park Avenue.

O PARADISO

Cartier, hunting for China, found
    the polar bear, "big as a cow and white as a swan,"
and wapiti with antlers like stiff ferns;
    plunged into Canada, observed the smaller tribes
of animals, replacements for the vanished plush
    of a spent world, and copper-colored chiefs
wrapped carelessly in the deep silk
    of badger, marten, vixen, and mink,
while Tudor monarchs straddling tired thrones
    invaded monastaries, pawed at creaking shelves
for copes and chasubles outlined with fur.
    French nobles grieved to see
their sable-lined nightgowns grow thin—
    took heart when Cartier's first cargo came
gleaming to port; sent out fresh hunters:
    the beaver-eyed Champlain, and *coureurs de bois*
to rampage in primeval woods
    where thirsty Hurons, munching birds,
delivered raw, red kingdoms in exchange
    for fire sloshing in a drunken cup.
The Dutch sent Hudson sailing to an inland bay
    whose roadless shores shook with the gloss
and weight of beasts, enough to clothe a continent
    of dukes, freebooters, merchants, priests:
and, rounding all, awash with broken flowers,
    the fertile, green, and whale-backed sea.

TRAPPER'S REPORT

They are domestic, faithful to their families,
    often work by moonlight,
    clerks and engineers in brisk overcoats,
    wearing keen incisors between wind-puffed cheeks,
    comedians of poplars and ponds,
    lovers of calculus
    and the long blue sums of water,

subject, by nature, to seasons
of lightning and frost
but pitching always above muddy foundations
their precise households
with porches as round
as the white hearts of birches.

They are captured easily in winter
in their domed cities.
When the light comes in with the hunter's axe,
and the bedroom floor—draped for darkness—
dazzles and blinks,
they run on their shoeless feet
to the sudden window,
confused by so early an April
and by the steep noose slung
around a low throat.

Hauled into day
(out of the dusky, two-story chamber
mattressed with summer and sleep,
clean as dead wheat,
and mumbling with babies),
their whiskers sweat,
beaded like a red abacus.
   They are full of blood
   when slit down the belly
   from neck to crotch
   and also on the inside of each leg
   to the center cut,
      the outer garment then peeled off
      both ways toward the spine
      and stretched on an oval frame,
      the guard hairs plucked
      to leave, brown-rayed and warm,
      a breathless velvet hung
      against the white and ever-naked wind.

COSTUME BOOK (Excerpt Two)

In summer, even chiefs went bare,
though seldom without the pointed jewels
of claws strung into necklaces,
or clacking halos of dead teeth
strung through their black and dancing hair.

Beaten hides of bison kept out the cold,
and their swift horns, headgear for warriors,
blazed like new moons turned into bone,
or served as flagons for an antelope's blood,
while the cosmetic bear, crowded with fat,
supplied his oozing brilliantine
to blaze on scalps and in a stone lamp's
rancid flame.
        Oar-shaped, the beaver's tail
flapped from the jerking hems of skirts,
while the eagle's hollowed wings
became a puffing painter's flute,
tube for pigments blown like colored smoke
against the borrowed skins of elk and deer
coaxed into shuffling, human shapes—
   but all forgiving, propitiated by prayer,
   their furless spirits tumbling in the palm
   of a great father overhead;
        even the fawn, weeping;
even the caribou, his sinews stretched
through the harsh needle's eye; even the parrot
plucked of his gaudy sleeves,
the puma stripped down to her steaming heart,
the ornamental porcupine—martyrs,
but reconciled, knowing the need
of naked Sioux and shivering Cherokee,
the shaman's quest of rattle, pouch, and rib,
and hearing always, above the arrow's gasp,
the ritual grunt of brute apology.

JOHN JACOB ASTOR

John Jacob Astor, with a pack of Indian goods upon his back,
wandered from the Indian trail, got lost in the low grounds
at the foot of Seneca Lake in the inclement night, wandered amid
the howl and rustling of wild beasts, until almost morning,
when he was attracted by the light of an Indian cabin . . .

Contemporary report

He had no love of wilderness,
endured its weeds and waste and creaking stars
for the sake of what it held
transmutable to gold;
learned Indian dialects,
survived bad food, cold nights, and lice,
charmed squatting chiefs
with music from his flute,
a German Pan with tuftless ears,
his feet stoutly enclosed in common shoes.

  Indian light amid the howl
  and rustling of wild beasts,
  the beaver huddled in her trap,
  one foot almost gnawed free—
  three paws left to dance upon
  to the trills of Jacob's metal reed.

  His mind moved
  to its own sharp tunes,
  past clubs and snares
  to cosmopolitan earth:
  plots and parcels of real estate—
  lots in lower Manhattan
  purchased "for a song"
  (and currency from pelts)
  in the same year
  George Washington,
  awkward on a New York balcony,
  became the president
  of town and coast and wilderness

and the bright-haired multitude of beasts
sparkling beyond the hum of mud
in savage city streets.

Triggers and shot he left to others,
mountain men brawling through thunder and spit
in pursuit of trails, prime pelts, and squaws,
and a dipper of whiskey. Their knives
were sharp as the young moon's edge,
and they left their dung in the forests
among droppings of grizzly and fox and lynx,
boasted of bears larger than mountains,
fought claw to claw with wolf and cougar,
split gut and groin without a shudder,
hollered hills down, picked their teeth with cactus,
grew great beards, swaggered like trees
in blizzards, stared into campfires
with smoke-stung eyes,
                              sometimes fearful of shadows
and of certain dreams in which cubs smiled
behind the dead fortress of their mother,
and a porcupine, kerosene-drenched and lighted,
        its stiff clothes on fire
        (sport for trapper, lumberjack, and scout),
        climbed an endless pine forever
        until its bumbling torch went out.

Rich, he sailed steerage to England
to sell his harvest;
shivered below decks,
recalled an earlier voyage
(the flutes now abandoned—for a good price),
the heat of executives overhead,
swaddled himself in the memory of money made
and money to come,
        Sarah's dowry and her shrewd hands
        on fur or flesh or cabbages.

Returned. Counted his profits,
watched her fingers chuckle
among receipts and dividends.
    The million-faceted wink of gold
    shone in her eyes, gave such warmth
    even in winter, there was no need
    to squander funds on extra coal.

Played with his children,
but carried a wound
from his firstborn and namesake—
    idiot, imbecile, whatever he was,
something strange, nodding and lisping
in a private upper room.

    Invested in Greenwich Village wastes,
    and Harlem's distance-burdened hills,
    extended his realm, by land, beyond the Northwest's river-roar
    to Canada; to the Indies and Canton, by sea,
    ships creaking with dead cargoes,
    defying embargo laws and slippery foam.

Tried to forget the noon-raw stench
of the Black Forest butcher shop,
and his grudging apprenticeship
to hanks of suet, sinews, dripping horns;
longed for prestige,
persuaded one daughter to accept
a foreign nobleman's desire,
then spent a fortune (nicked by pain)
pursuing help in health resorts and spas
for whatever moral ache Eliza found
in a royal bed;
    provided a proper funeral,
    sailed home through a hurricane shock of waves,
        offered the captain one thousand dollars,
            five thousand, ten,
                for a safe harbor—anywhere—
        was saved by the subsiding wind
        but not from the smirks of fellow passengers,

nor from the messenger at the dock.
Sarah's plump heart, also, was still,
    as the hearts of beavers left to rot
    where they were tossed in red and steaming hills.

Perceived an end to easy furs:
too many creatures killed,
too many worms with spinning mouths
replacing brilliant pelts with shining threads;
and his sea-battered colony, Astoria,
itself becoming a skeleton.
    Sold his interest, turned toward glitter of real estate,
    doubled and tripled his towering gold,
    commissioned a book to glorify his name,
    built his own castle, Astor House,
    foreclosed mortgages with contempt,
    bought and sold
    until his passionate empire rose like a great tomb
    above the dust and drift of lesser lives.

Grew old. Grew gray. Grew thin,
though buffered by multi-million layers of fat
stored up in Wall Street vaults;
fretted about his fragile bones and breath
and his title, "Old Skinflint,"
bestowed by popular consent.
    Went bundled in glorious furs.
    Had horses, shining like machines,
    draw him through rain and sun and leaves
    (Whitman saw him once, gray gaze from under
    a broad-brimmed, beaver hat),
    fought death back as he had battled poverty,
    hired attendants (at a minimum wage)
    to toss him like a wrinkled acrobat
    on a taut blanket and so persuade
    his withered blood to circulate through wheezing veins.
    Saliva ran from a paralyzed lip as from a liquid spool.
    At meals, a servant, uniformed,
    guided food to the quivering mouth and gut.

In time he lived on human milk,
sucked life from the breasts
of a wet nurse.
How much the cost of this?

In time, he died,
aged eighty-six,
thin as the bones
of little animals
hollowed by the wind,
empty as a flute,
   but expensive . . .
      thirty millions worth of dust.

COSTUME BOOK (Excerpt Three)

> Most fun furs are fairly cheap and come from mass-produced
> animals, such as the rabbit and lamb, but on the fringes of the
> fun-fur vogue are such wild creatures as wolf, skunk, raccoon,
> lynx, and the more expensive and beautiful spotted cats.
> *The New Yorker,* May 20, 1967

The more exotic, flower-stenciled beasts,
blood still drying to garnets on their fur,
are flown direct; leopard, jaguar, and ocelot
brought on steep wings to cutting rooms
where a scent of death, like scorched hair, clings,
and yet is beaded with the armpit stench of swamps.

  The leaf-splotched gold of eight Somali leopards
  is needed for one coat, silent on its hanger
  in the bedroom closet's motionless night,
  while special hunters race to find more beasts
  whose soft rosettes, made popular by Jacqueline,
  are coveted by other widows, wives, and debutantes.

  Of the smaller Felidae,
  no larger than the moaning shapes,

that haunt our rotting alleyways
in search of fish heads shining like old tin,
twenty-five must go to make a shivering wrap
against the wind in limousines or ships.

The cheetah's silk, though it does not wear as well
as the leopard's flowing cloth, is "sportier"
among those who peddle such intense brocades.
Tiger skin, indelibly marked
by shafts of light and shade,
needs a special female type
to bear its wild embroidery—
    skinny, tall, with a feline slant
    around the eyes, cheekbones, or teeth.

Mountains lions, for all their grace, are difficult,
the color, like a red-brown sunset, harsh;
recommended strictly for casual dress—
ski slopes, winter golf, a northern beach,
or race tracks when the chill is deep enough.

Each year the stock goes down, the price goes up.
Broker and hunter sniff at dwindling maps,
tiptoe down trails toward things that flash like spotted jewels
but quake and flee, though never fast enough
to dodge the bullet's yearning arc.

    The ocelot, bright black and gold,
    is stacked in heaps, torn from Bolivia
    and breath. The snow leopard, stretched and groomed,
    makes a rug so deep, the appraiser's fingers
    sleep in it, reluctant to wake;
    so warm, it seems still wrapped around a heart
    beating against the blue Himalayan frost.
    The jaguar, mottled with pansies,
    hangs from a hook beside the lynx and headless wolf,
    all thirst and pain removed,
    insured against mildew, moths, and thieves.

Art is required to stitch invisible seams,
mend bullet scars, design the whole
to glorify a mannequin with plastic eyes
staring at lovers from her transparent cage,
the price tag delicately concealed.

   The salesmen smile, inspect a credit card,
   then wrap with ease, and tenderly bind
   the supple prize—perfumed and plucked and sleek—
   remote from death, it seems, of any kind.

Sky Diver

Grotesque, jumping out
like a clothed frog, helmet and glasses,
arms and legs wading the sky,
feet flapping before the cloth flower opens;
then suspended, poised,
an exclamation point upside-down,
and going down, swaying over corn and creeks
and highways scribbled
over the bones of fish and eagles.

There is the interim between air and earth,
time to study steeples
and the underwings of birds going over,
before the unseen chasm,
the sudden jaw open and hissing.

Lying here after the last jump
I see how fanatic roots are,
how moles breathe through darkness,
how deep the earth can be.

Tree Service

Jockey, juggler, rider of ropes and leaves,
climber with metal thorns nailed to his feet,
he kicks dust back, stomps upward on his spurs
until his yellow bump hat bobs and gleams
among the antlers of a dying beast.

I could not save it, and it hung too near
with blackening horns aimed for the house,
but I am bothered by this hired shape
going up through the dead lace of boughs
that never felt a sharper tooth than sleet.

Yet I must back him since his life is pitched
against an overgrown and staglike head
assembling ruin above my roof,
though dreading the first severed branch
and its steep plunge.
                             It falls, scattering rot
like chaff from a broken star; more sky moves in
but I miss the reaching claw. A hoof goes next—
it paced for years above my fires and mist—
and I perceive how easily space grows
around a saw.
                    He swings and sears,
agile as a toy, the round hat floating
like a crown. I feel an office worker's awe
for his hard bustling thighs and arms.

Only the rough, round trunk remains.
A portion falls, the sound heart glowing red
against a litter of gray, scattered veins,
witness to how communication failed
between the blowing top and the dark nerves
that worked in ignorance to feed a dying crest.

The saw is still at last, and still the great stump
throbs and shines, the hidden taproot busy as before,
cell, core, and tissue storing useless fat.
The sky looks bare. The wind is high and keen;
it draws a knife against my back.

Avalanche

The drift descends like rattling dust
from step and bough and lofty weed,
flaps in the wind, stamps on the deck,
litters the eaves with seed and spore
and pods as dry as old canoes,
until the house creaks in the flow
sent down to us by teeming hills.

All day, all year, and in cold dreams
I fight an avalanche of lives
swarming in silk, brooding in bark,
intent on sprouting anywhere—
along the sink, beneath the door,
out of the chimney's leafless mouth,
from every wrinkle, crack, or pore,
armpit or furrow, crevice or gut,
and the grit of eyelids closed too long.

I wake up often in the dark,
alerted by a sudden field
of thistles pressed against a wall,
and smell the heat of each dry torch,
or hear beneath my silent desk
the wild cucumber's spiny purse
drag an inch forward, pause, and scrape
another step. I try for sleep
but the pillow has its nettles up,
the room is rank with sweat and thorn.

Each dawn, each day, I rise and dress,
clutch clumsy tools, use my own hands
to rake the dross from lilac beds,
spy out odd corners, scour and sweep,
uproot all vines that choke the lives
I want to keep; and yet I know
how soon, some night, the drift will flow,
pile up, and fill my seedless eyes.

Foundations

Houses need air underneath.
Otherwise, wood rots.
I have been alert,
knocked out the smothering blocks
false builders built.

This pickaxe has a beak
like an iron pelican.
My hands have calluses and wounds,
small price to pay
for wind beneath the floor
and a breathing roof
above all creatures there
who keep so much of the dark for us.

Deities

One wrinkled god
stands beside the scorpion's tail,
half holds it up, instructs the uncertain head
which way to turn
toward what is dark or wet.
Another holds the trout's jaws wide
until the hook arrives.

Some ride with camels
(spit from sandy throats),
warble in nests with mice,
wake with the junco,
put fists in cyclones,
peel the long bark from birches,
push at grass,
pry open the sluggish iris,
teach rain to tap-dance
and the lightning how to leap
like nerves in a furnace.

One, stunted, climbs
the neck of the giraffe.
One, squinting, has made the cat
and us
see more of night than we require.

Hunter's Cabin

The deer horns on my fence,
sharp as the skeleton of a hand,
turn green in winter rain,
part moss, part bone,
part something else not fastened there
but running fast through loam and spit
and sparks of blood.

I half expect such things to sprout,
become a stem or leaf,
or suddenly a savage head,
the nostrils warm and steep,
ears strung with hair,
the brown teeth arched.

Wind plucks the chicken wire
like a hoof,
and the horns clack.
A forehead gleams and grows
in my black woods.
The large, dead eyes look out.

Séance

Something, somebody, is trying to speak through me—
ant or ape or a great-grandmother,
perhaps a voice even older,
perhaps the sea, perhaps a throat in the sea,
perhaps a shape without eyes or thumbs,
dust, maybe, or some ancient crab
hobbling sidewise on his skinless knuckles.

When I try to speak for myself
there is a crackle and a hum.
Bones appear in my voice and break
and another voice rattles.

I have wakened at night
and heard weeds chanting on my pillow
or birdlike things with notes as bright as new straw,
and a creature very wrinkled and huge
groaning like a mountain with a wound in its side.

The Sleep of Animals

There is no way to enter into it.
They are enclosed, infolded,
rolled deep in their own darkness.
There is no way to follow their visions,
neither those of the horse, the sloth, the tiger,
not even the household mascot.
Only by a quiver of a haunch,
a twitch of an ear or whisker,
or sometimes the white of an eye rolling
can one guess that they dream at all.

I shall never know
what perfumed field the pony grazed,
what hammock the sloth invented,
what orange memories fed the tiger;
nor they
what jungles I explore,
what hearts I savor,
in my own night,
as deep as any.

Cellar

That time I tumbled into the dark—
   tilt, plunge, and cry
   through a trap door left open
   in a trusted pantry floor—

      that descent, child-hair streaming,
      into a kingdom of potatoes
      (their tall eyes sprouting upward
      like pale rockets),
      dried onions, squash, cold fists of cabbages,
      carrots hanging like withered darts,
      preserves and relish winking
      from provident shelves,
but the dust alive and daintily clawed:

      that moment of plunging through linoleum
      embossed with faded birds
      (the bitter smell of wind
      or coal or something darker
      hunched inside a box),
      the gasp of arrival on hardened earth,
      then the quick leap up
      the raw wood stairs
      toward a living room with lights still on—
         being saved from rot
         and breathing mice
         and the crimson stars of tomatoes sliced
      and staring out of glass—
resurrected, full of heart . . .

      but now on deeper nights
      a different void
      below the humpbacked dreams,
      and no light left
      except a clock's dim hands
      that pace my gray,
      yet climbing, breath.

Message

Something has caught in my throat,
neither frog nor bone,
more like a fork
that tastes of alum,
or a stone that has lived in fire,
possibly a jewel
(the ruby's red glass furnace),
perhaps a diamond, unpolished
(white eye in darkness),
or simply my own breath
grown jagged,
trapped between speech and silence.

There is no surgeon for this,
or not one near enough
this high-pitched place
whirled round by mountains
and the wind's unfettered voice.

I shall learn sign language
but even then the stone
or fork or fire, desire's impediment,
will make my hands stutter.

Consider this when next I call
or try to signal
across mesas, thunder, gulfs,
and the garrulous crosses
of telephone poles.

Evening might be the best time,
when I am a silhouette—
or some deep morning
when, in stillness,
you could catch the beat—
the clear and strenuous tone—

of that fixed voice
where my heart swings
in its round perch,
alone, yet not alone.

As It Is

for Laura

Wife love, father love, love of an old dog,
whatever love it is—if it is love—
is twined through stress
(disease, a wound, a grinding debt)
into so tight a skein
the leanest filament seems gross:
    threads in light bulbs;
    split ends of human hair;
    the close, red conduits
    through which blood creaks and booms
    in echo chambers of motels,
    deserted chairs, black trains,
    or just a dusty seashell in a drawer,
    curved like a porcelain ear.

Things shake and sigh with it—
roofs, knobs, and doors—
and common neighbors coming home,
seeing an ambulance,
a wandering child,
a foreign license plate,
an empty yard,
or furniture stacked outside
like varnished bones.

It toils and sleeps;
it wrestles and cooks meals,
copes with mountains, dust cloths, tears;
carries out trash, seeks interviews,
limps through heat; scrubs, burrows, cries,
boils water, holds a dying paw,
       does what it does
       to keep pain back awhile—if it is pain—
       as it must be
       if it is love.

From the Diggings

In 1919, archeologists digging among grave mounds
along an ancient Roman road in Luxembourg
discovered a crystal phial containing tears shed
two thousand years before.

The dust is known and filled with teeth,
dead hairpins, urns, a breastplate scabbed
by preening rot. In the hot drift
the trowels burn, and picks, long-eyed as pelicans,
chip through the dark,
unearthing common things
until, just where the grave swell ends—
a gleam. A wink. A something caught
and stoppered up like rain;
salt, grief, and residue intact.

No burgomaster, serf, or slave,
not even a huntsman trimmed in fur,
possessed such dainty sepulchres.
    Some queen with sodden lids
    preserved her pain
    in that slim vault;
    some melancholy prince—
unless upon one desperate night
a jester stole into his monarch's room
and, armed with crystal, teased a royal ape
until that clanking beast, like any king,
wept from his tiny, blood-swept eyes.

Water Strider

This stranger on slanted legs
straddles an inch of water,
adjusts his pointed heels
and twirls upon his shadow;
for his shadow is always with him,
hanging from his belly,
its green face looking up
to his leaning face above it.
His other shadow, down deep,
hangs from the yellow sun
and lights up each blue foot,
flat in a whirling sandal.

Self-portrait

In this sketch I am in a canoe
as silver as a young moon,
and the water is so still
it hums with the pickerel's delicate teeth.
The water is so deep
the sunfish's lantern burns out,
and my hook is a steel question mark
hanging upsidedown in all the night
the lake hauls to itself
from forests, scum, or passing rot.

I am wearing a white shirt,
the sleeves pushed up,
and at my feet a jug of wine rolls
like a round, glass child.
My tackle box is trim,
and a painted bobber winks
above the barb designed
to lure some hunger underneath.

It is all deceit—
the boat, the gaff hook, net, and knife,
props only for a chance to watch, alone,
the light and wind and perchless sky.
I dread the least tug at the line,
the gasping weight, the wounded throat,
but the risk of blood, as everywhere, is great.

Tulip Fancier

They are self centered,
concentrated as knuckles,
lie stacked and sorted
like paper-wrapped skulls
in the bins beneath my house:
Darwins, Rembrandts, Mendels,
time-clocks inside them
whirring at their round, dry foreheads.

This one, in love with habit,
is determined to be pink
with a precise pathway of silver
on the tongue of each petal;
this one is concerned only
with orangeness and feathered edges.
That one, brooding in a corner,
is obsessed with becoming vermilion.

Even in the slow pendulum of summer,
out of their nests, there is a hum.
Something fanatic is there,
and the mouthless bulbs,
gorged with the fat of what was
stem and flower,
simmer with waiting.

Judgment Day

The slug was too near
the fire of weeds and old wood,
a low, bullet-shaped thing,
his invisible gut
pink with my choice begonias.

Still, I lifted him,
gray turd of life,
and tossed him toward salvation,
though it will earn me no points
when my red turn comes.

Solo, Non-Stop

Donald Crowhurst set out from England in 1968 to sail
non-stop around the world. His radio messages told
of a record-smashing voyage before his boat was found
adrift, empty, in mid-ocean. He had been sailing in circles
for eight months when apparently he threw himself
into the sea.

My lie was my gift
made out of lost stars
and a circling ghost of shores
never reached.

My boat, too, was false,
warped and fragile from the start,
a brittle pod
consumed by spray
and waves greener than hills,
while my compass needle spun
like devil-dust,

But
think of my messages
to you snug at home—
signals of a hero
wrapped in sharks and thunder,
pursuing always
the prize that jigged
beyond your safe, slow meadows—

each of you sustained,
sailing imaginary oceans,
ever achieving
in my spendthrift shadow:

smashers of records,
dreamers, inheritors of islands
and headlines,
  smoking pipes in your bedrooms,
  waiting in the underground,
  or dressing for dinner,
  safe from my skull's blue drowning.

Iowa Biography

for Josie

The horizon was hers beyond the barn
and running fields. Heaven, assured,
hung where the church spire reached
to hold up half the stretching sky
above stork-regiments of corn.
Yet, something underfoot and ripe—
ground cherries, squash, red gift of fallen plums—
gave faith an extra nourishment
and her wide, working hands
a chance to reverence earthy things:
chicks yellower than dandelions,
roundness of apples and Mason jars,
milk pails, loud churns—and bread:
almost it seemed, each time,
Christ newly risen
out of yeast's strange coils and springs,
essential miracle for child and child
shouting across the crowded wind.

These shouts had an eager way of going,
though echoes clung to porch and swing.
Earth, in age, brought different sounds.
The windmill gasped that turned the air
through eighty years of days.
Corn was louder, darker, at dusk,
then changed to just a dream of sound
in a rented room where silence grew,
and only the clock knew a cricket tune.

Ghosts thumped white fists on the waiting door;
lost bones of chicks or children blew
on a siren's wail. Against some living visitor,
blizzards spun wagons of unwanted lace,
and pain kept time with her tatting hands.

Still, roots with keen inverted spires
thrust down to hold the world awhile.
Horizons dimmed to a waning clock
on the dresser where rose-scented beads
dozed within drawers beside chocolate hearts,
a fading garden of photographs,
holiday cards wrinkled like husks,
a Bible, trinkets, a ball of twine—
harvest, oh, harvest, harvest!

Drumcliffe: Passing By

> Cast a cold Eye
> On Life, on Death.
> Horseman, pass by!
>
> W. B. Yeats's tombstone

It was rain and green and always rain,
and the May cold spilling through rock walls
into bone-walls and brain, caught in the folds
of clothing and breath, dripping where farmers walked
like swimmers trapped in weedy boots,
hissing on hedges and dogs and death.
Rain has its home there, building ditches, ruins,
and green-haired wives.
　　　　　　　　At Yeats's grave,
under a black umbrella's roof,
I understood how rarely blue exists
and how, no doubt, his poet's skull
lies packed with moss in less than thirty years
beneath his plain, admonishing stone.

The rooks were noisy rags in blowing trees.
Swallows, as neat as bats, dived through mist
for their winged food.
　　　　　　　No horseman I,
but still a rider through rain and green
and dusk, casting a cold eye.

Greenwich Mean Time

SOLAR TIME

> The time unit most commonly employed since prehistoric times
> is the apparent daily circuit of the sun.
>
> —*Columbia Encyclopedia*

The sun—
   that rolling hill of fire,
   that furance hung past blistering ice—
     from it our ticking lives suspend:
     hearts, crops, and clocks,
     appointments, graduations, games;
     even the cricket
     with his bronze leather thighs
     leans on its soundless swing
     around our rooted world.

The sun—
   that fist of sparks,
   that furious star—
     on it the rattling mouse depends,
     the gull that seeks
     blue elevators in the wind,
     and the deep whale lounging
     in basements beyond light or sight
     but still hauled by the sun,
     and locked in time.

Children regret the fever of its going,
then race against insidious dusk
to carry their lengthening shadows home.

     The cocktail hour diminishes and dies;
     a last lamp surrenders to the dark;
     and we, the daily circuit done,
     turn to the wall and strive again
     for the solstice of blind sleep.

STAR TIME

Khufu, builder of the Great Pyramid,
had a "telescope" installed within the walls.

The stone spy hole, lensless, immovable,
a stationary eye set in a tomb,
was aimed to catch the northern star
at its bright work—a seeming firefly
that moved mechanically as if on wires
some cunning engineer had strung
across the upsidedown abyss
of reachless sky.
              Slaves snored beside
the salt-gray rocks their backs had hauled
through aisles of sweat; only a king had time
to gaze at splendid trinkets overhead:
blue chandeliers, red pendants, pearls,
a comet like a long-tailed, blazing fish.
Each night he knelt beneath his crown,
eyes pressed to that crude orifice,
his funeral chamber at his back.

On every cloudless watch, the star swung past
the dazzled aperture, its punctual glow
turning time into something measurable as light
though the room was black, as blood was black
when it darkened in the sand-pocked air
where workers burst their lungs and died.
The sepulchre at night was cool
and at the instant when the tail
of Ursa Minor flashed
above the limestone telescope
its ice glow made a sudden silver run
down royal hair and cheek and lip.
He felt the chill and prayed
to Osiris in whose hot loins
the sun's seeds rode.
              The star steered on
and he was moved to think

what other power, when he was gone,
could put a similar will on space.

His mummy sleeps, like some thick, paper worm.
Even the eyes are gone
that saw Polaris stride
on its invisible stilts
above that mammoth, pointed grave.
Time, metered out, he found
was less starlight than rot
in spite of spices stuffed
within the scooped-out cavity
where once his lungs and liver toiled
to keep his dreaming breath alive.

The heart, for all its lengthy bath
in priestly brines
became a thimbleful of air
not even archeologists can weigh.
There, as in lesser shrines,
only dust—some teeth—
some scraps of hair—
emit a starless gleam
beneath a finite flashlight's ray,
and heaven (all heavens anywhere)
remains light-years,
night-years, away.

GREGORIAN ADJUSTMENT, 1582

George Washington's birthday, February 11,
Old Style; February 22, New Style

The equinox was out of joint.
In twelve hundred years plus fifty-seven
the trusted calendar went awry,
developing an error of ten days,
so nothing matched.

Leaves bloomed too late;
birds nested in blank boughs;
even roosters were crowing out of tune.

Pope Gregory on his stiff throne
bent brow to fist,
attempting to reel time back
to something rational and true.
From prayer and thought he ruled
ten strumpet days must be tossed out
upon the dump heap of eternity,
the daily reckoning rectified.

Time is a racer and a sloth.
The Pope's chill bones
were tapestry
by the time his rectification came
to the American Colonies
and caught Ben Franklin
out of time . . .
ten days plus one
(a leap year's maverick sprint)
to be deducted from the total sum
of trips abroad, tomes, kites, and love.
Franklin was one who treasured sleep,
regretted those sweet hours lost;
yet philosophy with him ran deep,
and time was but a sieve, he knew,
through which one must expect a leak.

Our founding fathers took in stride
corrections of inevitable flaws.
Some losses had to be.
Birthdays were hustled into line,
adjustments made for wages lost,
new dates assigned to deaths or anniversaires.
But still the gap yawns there:
eleven days of expurgated history.

INDICATIONS OF TIME

Announcement of the sun
and birds quilting shadows
while the clock sits,
black hands folded;
recital of cars in hurried evening,
and a bull-horned moon
with a blue cape behind it;
pink and terror
of the day's shell-breaking,
and the thin thighs of crabs
designing the seashore;
sigh of the machine
with its iron pulse straining
and the nurse's wrench
seeking to soothe it;
thunder of the nerve
with its red tooth waking;
stillness of time
with two arms extended.
A bone sits on the clock
and the bone is ticking.

MIDNIGHT SAVING TIME

How to deal with these hours,
alone under the ceiling's black canopy
while the clock multiplies its two fingers
into ten, eleven, twelve,
cracks its knuckles at midnight,
builds an exclamation point,
then starts all over again?

My pillow smells of smoke,
skin lotions, gin, and something wilder,
almost out of time,
as when some other anxious head, on rock
or weeds, rolled in a vision

of a world being born
out of an animal stink and splendor;
invented an upright spine
and walked this way
and to this room
to stand in his primordial hair,
hand grasping mine.

Cousin, your cave was better than you knew.
Except for you, we might have stayed
beyond the mind's chill blast,
the wheel's hot, greasy stride,
scratching our fleas
but wrapped in snores
beside a warm, exhausted mate,
our only clock a waterfall or gonging moon.

I await, awake, the gadgetries of day—
the percolator plugged into my veins,
the toaster clicking with my borrowed nerves,
and then the traffic's grinding games,
my blood a pawn, all hours blown
down office shafts and streets and bars
until, again, the pitch and pall of night.

You with your shaggy eye and reach
would have saved at least some bone from these.
I munch on air, not knowing how to use
either my darkness or my light.

LIFETIME

I am at the age when you grow ten years older in one year . . .
Ionesco

The slowing down, the lag and the slack
on common stairs and hills, are all external
like warts that blossom overnight
in the mirror, and the white wires that sprout

from nostril and eyebrow. Within,
dark within the coverings of skin and cloth,
deep within the trappings of bone and blood,
there is a runner racing ever faster
to gain a leap on the lip of the grin
where the world slips, slides, ends.

How nimble the inward chase,
how ardent the gray-haired sprinter
though he stumble over a thread
or have hands as unsteady as water;
how yet he pursues the instant of breath
between the cry into light
and the cry into darkness,
and the time-stop machine always ticking.

The past is my runner's cape.
It flows out behind me like a train
of dust—
              though there are sparks in it
burning with rubies and roses,
flash of warm arms, great moons rising,
scent of grass gathered into green curtains,
mirages of mouths, eyes, swimmers, sleepers,
fragrance of voices,
memories of lust satisfied
(lovely as the wind's firelight on mountains),
but all of it a streaming trail of dust
blown backward as I race ever faster—
how the dawns rush by me—
to escape my own hunting shadow.

DATELINE: CALENDAR TIME

   The day begins with an imaginary line
drawn over the Pacific's tilt and boom,
invisible thread that knots the sun,
gossamer hurdle for flying fish,

unseen barrier through which ships pass
as through a horizontal ghost.

No ruler drew the dateline's rigid spine
across tumultuous earth and wave
except the ruler of the mind
with its lean edge.
Inflexible, imperious, it makes a boundary
between midnight and dawn,
governs the submarine's wet glide,
the airliner's takeoff and speed,
all trains, all barges, subways, cars,
and regulates the garbage truck's
arrival in a brittle street
where sleepers deep in inner rooms
pace their own dreams by that thin strand.

But breath-time, heart-time, circadian,
is finer than a dotted line.
Stretched taut on hemispheres within,
it knows precisely when the sun
swims into night, and how,
some hour, it will never rise again
in spite of travelers' clocks
or planes, or dolphins rainbowing across
a frail, fictitious wake
of what seems something like a dawn
but is in fact eternal dark.

ROUND-TRIP PASSENGER: JET TIME

No journey is to be undertaken lightly
whether over mountains, through meadows,
or into a tunnel that like a rifle barrel
has a distant, flickering eye of blue;
all can become, in an instant, fire.

Nor is the pattern always true
between one horizon and another,
the aim seldom being steady
but a conjunction of ascent and falling,
of unforeseen stars that must be followed,
of trestles broken, the train still howling onward;
or ships, even canoes, with a hidden fault—
some rivet askew, or only rot working
with its unheard singsong of patience.

For those on wings, the hazard is highest.
Time, where the keen jets scorch the sky,
whirls out of place, spins on its hub,
reels back, ahead, squats in a trance
until no passenger can trust his watch
or stammering pulse to know the hour.
Even the terminal clock can seem a liar
to travelers descending out of clouds—
those round, white blossomers,
those orchards drifing beyond touch
above fields copied, and revised,
from textbooks on geometry, the pages green,
or deserts spread like lion skins
between the wrinkled maps of streams.

To arrive at last, to take the risk
of stepping down from sunrise into dark
(since back where you took flight for home
dawn held its yellow sparkler up—
and there were passionate promises,
already lies though bold as the rifle's stare),
then to haul the midnight baggage out
from that time zone to this
and wade on jet-lag thighs
a ramp familiar as breath
but changed—steeper and narrower than you knew—
and suddenly perilous.

GREENWICH MEAN TIME

Begin with zero here on this low hill
where the Thames, broad-backed and brown,
ferries its load of yachts and excrement
past the invisible but Prime Meridian,
that hatchery in which time spawns
swift minnow seconds fattening in a leap
toward minutes, hours, years,
a century, millennium, eternity.

The monster has a voice like a tin bird
clucking across the short-wave band.
It chirps, it cheeps, it keens
out of the plastic cage that amplifies
the smallest whisper the transmitter makes;
invades the bedroom, closet, bath,
the lisping church, the conference room.
A human ventriloquist speaks for it:
"At the sound of the tone
it will be five hours . . ." (six? twelve? none?)
"four minutes, Greenwich Mean Time."

Begin with zero where
the red-faced infant yowls at birth;
the mausoleum perches with its crypt;
the bombers dive and drop their howling loads
to deliver the final cipher, death;
and here, within this interval,
where all of us (hearing the countdown
from every screen) seek ways, meantime,
to live within our limited means.

BEYOND GREENWICH

I am going to go down into the tides
where the moon swings
and time is as dark as the shark's fin
wrinkling above a white spool of water.

I am going to learn
from the cold tunes of congers
what ocean time is
and how it booms over
the announcement of bells
on a liner's deck.

I shall plunge through
the green gut of the abyss,
far below serpent or urchin,
down where blackness and silence
make midnight seem a blaze of operas.

I shall dive deep, deeper.
I shall become a fish of sorts.
I shall wear a skin of icicles.
I shall avoid all hooks
though my teeth be as sharp
as the cutting edge of the wings of swans.